Wolfsbane

Rachel Rawlings

Rachel Rawlings

Wolfsbane
A Maurin Kincaide Novel

Written by
Rachel Rawlings

Published in the United States by:

R Squared Publishing

http://www.rachelrawlings.com

Even a man who is pure in heart

And says his prayers by night

May become a wolf

When the Wolfsbane blooms

And the moon is full and bright

~Gypsy Poem

Chapter One

I woke in a cold sweat to the sound of heavy gun fire. I grabbed the Retaliator from the empty side of the bed and bolted out of my room. My front door was open and I was out in the little stairway that led to my third floor walk up before I was awake enough to realize there was no danger. My first clue should have been Conry- a Cwnn Anfwnn, gift from my father and personal guard "dog"- just rolling over and burying his head beneath his massive paws.

The sound of grenades and Dempsey's voice coming up the stairs told me it was just my new neighbor playing COD Zombies with the TV full blast at three o'clock in the morning *again.* I was still in boy shorts and a tank top but I didn't bother to go back in my apartment to change. He'd seen me in less. I stormed down the flight of stairs to Cash's apartment with my sword in hand.

"It's going on four in the morning! Turn that shit off or I'll send some real zombies to your apartment!" I yelled while I pounded on the door.

How the guy on the first floor slept through it I'll never know. But it had been me stomping on my floor and banging on Cash's door every night for the last month.

"What's the big deal? I figured a fanger like you would be used to staying up late." Cash casually replied upon opening the door.

"You can be such a jerk." I said with more venom than the insult commanded.

"Jerk? That's the best you could come up with?" Cash said through his laughter.

"Oh, I'm sorry. I'm not at my wittiest when I wake up to the sound of World War III at three in the morning." I said tartly.

"It's Modern Warfare, not World War III." He smirked.

I rolled my eyes. "I'm not the only other person who lives here you know. I can only imagine what it sounds like downstairs. The poor guy probably has to sleep with ear plugs in." I scolded.

"Mike works third shift. He doesn't get home until after seven in the morning. " He was still smirking.

"He's only lived here for like three weeks and I haven't even talked to him. You two are what, like best friends already?" I asked, irritated.

"What can I say? People just like me better than you." He was past smirking and into a full grin.

I probably shouldn't have but I couldn't help myself. I swung the Retaliator around until the tip of the blade pressed against his Adam's apple. "Just turn the TV down or we'll see how good of a gamer you are without your thumbs."

I stomped away. "And stop staring at my ass." I said as I started up the steps. If the challenge for

Alpha of the Salem pack didn't happen soon Roul was going to start getting wake up calls at three in the morning. I didn't know what the holdup was anyway. He was too busy to help us with the Inquisitors and the demon they unleashed a few weeks ago because of his "pack business" and now it's delay, delay, delay. It's been unusually quiet in Salem but I haven't had a decent night's sleep in four weeks because of my new neighbor.

Well, it wasn't all Cash's fault. Aidan had a little something to do with it - too bad it was just talking. Aidan made his feelings for me clear but was still insisting we take our time. Vampires could be very patient. Having spent most of my life living more like a "norm" than an immortal I found it infuriating. He wanted to be sure the effects of Mahalia's spell were gone. I assured him that any feelings I had for Oberon died the minute I found out he hadn't. I thought I had killed him, pulling too much power through the tie that bound us. In order to save himself, he broke the connection and the false feelings for him Mahalia had spelled into my heart.

I tried on more than one occasion to convince Aidan that I hadn't felt more like myself since Mahalia's magic had been broken. That had been a monumental waste of time. It takes powerful magic to control someone's heart and mind, he explained during one of our all night conversations. I had had other things on my mind, things that didn't involve so much talking. I used all my feminine wiles to persuade him - unsuccessfully. He was convinced lingering magic would try to latch itself onto the next person to vie for my affections. His conviction to determine my true feelings made for more than one long and frustrating night. Not to mention my temper was becoming increasingly short. Which might explain why I was down here threatening to cut fingers off my irritating neighbor's hands.

"No kiss good night?" Cash asked sarcastically.

I didn't bother with a response. Cash was one of the few people I knew who had as many smart ass comebacks as me. If I didn't walk away we'd be going at each other until the sun came up.

"How about a kiss for good luck then?" He called out as I was half way up the stairs. "The challenge is tonight."

I turned around slowly. How weird was that? I was just ranting to myself about how Roul was dragging his ass. If I didn't know better, I would have thought Weres had suddenly developed the ability to read minds. Thankfully they hadn't or my thoughts about Roul wouldn't have been the only thing Cash would have glimpsed. He didn't need any more ammunition when it came to aggravating my vampire. If Cash even suspected my frustration with Aidan it would be like arming a nuclear war head.

"The only lips she'll be kissing are mine, wolf." Aidan's voice carried up the stairway from the first floor. I'd hardly seen him over the last couple of weeks. Just hearing his voice sent shivers up my spine and I silently cursed him, knowing full well we wouldn't get further than second base again tonight.

I'm sure Cash knew he was there, hence the kiss comments but I hadn't been expecting him. So why had he suddenly shown up on my doorstep? Curiosity over his surprise visit quieted my suddenly raging hormones. He had been working every night on some new assignment that he couldn't talk about. It was starting to piss me off actually - not the constantly working part, the not knowing part. To be honest, my increasingly bad mood may have stemmed more from being out of the action than Aidan staying out of my bedroom. Sure, the time off from saving Salem from imminent danger was great. At first anyway, but it had been almost a month of peace and quiet. After only a week I found myself wishing for some sort of Armageddon. Whatever Aidan was working on seemed to be the cure for my doldrums - and pent up sexual energy - but Agrona had me on the sidelines with no intentions of letting me play in their vampire games.

Cash mumbled some vampire related insults as he shut his door. Aidan took my hand and led me up to my apartment.

"I didn't expect to see you tonight." I said after we got inside, trying to hide the desire for him in my voice.

"Did I interrupt something between you and the wolf?" He asked, a hint of jealousy in his voice.

"In his dreams." I said laughing.

"I wouldn't doubt it." He grumbled.

"Eewww." I shivered at the thought of Cash dreaming about me. More specifically me with him. It wasn't that Cash was totally repulsive I just didn't think of him like that. Ever.

"Do you think you could put on... something more than this the next time you pay Cash a visit." He gestured to my clothes - or lack thereof.

"Something tells me it's more than Cash that has you in a foul mood. What's going on Aidan?" I tried to hide the excitement in my voice.

I knew the lull in activity was too good to be true. It had been too quiet. Something big was happening. Finally! I was practically salivating and too my surprise it had less to do with my delicious vampire and more to do with the opportunity to use my sword.

"I'm going out of town." He said.

"What?" I asked, surprised and disappointed. That wasn't the something big I was expecting.

"It's the assignment I've been working on." He didn't elaborate.

"The one you can't talk about." I said, hoping he would suddenly feel overwhelmed with the need to tell me everything.

He just nodded. Damn it. What the hell was he working on?

"Can you at least tell me where you're going and for how long?" I didn't expect an answer.

"Reykjavik. I should be back in a couple of weeks." Aidan wasn't giving me any more than that. Being Council Liaison was not an all access pass to everything the Council was involved in. I didn't have to be a brain surgeon to figure out he was hunting someone. Aidan was the Cleaner. If he was traveling it was to chase down a naughty vampire, clean up their mess and convince them to behave. He could be very persuasive.

"I might have asked to tag along if it was somewhere a little warmer and with a little less snow than Iceland." I said, trying to sound like I didn't care he was leaving.

"Actually Greenland has more snow and ice. If it was possible for you to come with me I would have found a way to convince you." He pulled me into a hug.

"When are you leaving?" I asked his chest.

"Tonight, now. I was supposed to be at the airport already but I wanted to see you." He whispered against my neck, his fangs brushing against my skin.

"Don't start something you can't finish." I warned.

"I'm just trying to make an impression so you won't forget about me while I'm gone." He laughed.

"Our get me all worked up and leave me alone with an Alpha contender right down stairs. Aren't you worried that your fears about my feelings for you are right and that I might just latch on to the next eligible bachelor while you're gone?" I teased, as if that would happen. I was sure of my feelings for Aidan even if he wasn't. "Kidding, I'm just kidding." I said when his expression darkened.

"That's not funny." He was dead serious. His jealousy and anger suddenly a palpable thing.

"I'm sorry." I said and meant it. It was childish and potentially dangerous to send him off angry and distracted. "You know you have nothing to worry about where Cash is concerned but if it makes you feel better to hear it," I raised my fingers in the Girl Scout salute. "I promise I'll be on my best behavior while you're away. Scout's honor."

"You weren't a Girl Scout." He said, his anger and worry only slightly abated.

"Yes I was. Until the incident." I chuckled.

"The incident?" He asked.

"That's what my mother called it. Let's just say that was the last time she tried to assimilate me with the Norms." I hid the resentment behind my laughter.

He leaned in and kissed me gently on the lips. "I've got to go." His breath felt cool against my skin.

"You're already late. What's a few more minutes?" It was getting harder to ignore the carnal desire I had for this man and I wanted to reassure him it was only him I wanted. I pressed my body against his.

"Temptress." He laughed. His hands trailed along my arms, around my back until they cupped my ass. He pressed me closer to his body. "When I finally have you in my bed I will require more than a few minutes to ravage you properly." He let me go, distancing himself just enough to keep things from going further but not enough that I couldn't feel his desire for me. "I can't miss this flight. They won't hold the plane forever. Do you have any idea how difficult it is to arrange international travel for a vampire? It isn't like I can just take an aisle seat on a commercial flight."

"Well the over head compartment must be torture for a flight that long." I teased.

"Ha, ha. I'm hitching a ride with a friend on a vampire friendly jet but she has her own itinerary. If I'm not at Logan in forty-five minutes she's leaving without me." He explained.

"Oh my god, how do you stand it? A private jet, that is awful. I cannot believe the Council is forcing you to work under these conditions. You should start a union." I joked. "Wait, what? She?"

"You know you have nothing to worry about." Aidan said, throwing my own words back at me. "She's just the personal assistant of a long time friend. I wouldn't jeopardize what I have with you over a tryst in an airplane."

He gave me a quick kiss and was out the door before I could ask any more questions about his traveling companion. I tried to go back to sleep but thoughts of Aidan joining a vampire mile high club with some secretary fresh off the set of Mad Men made it damn near impossible. I envisioned him feeding from her, one thing would lead to another and she would be personally assisting him, so to speak. The sun was coming up by the time I finally fell asleep.

I woke up, for the second time, to Conry growling at my answering machine. 'At least it was a more reasonable hour', I thought as I glanced at my alarm clock. I laughed when I heard the voice coming through the speaker, amazed how Conry instinctively didn't like her. "Good boy." I said, scratching him behind his ears.

"I hope you're in the shower. I have never understood why you can't seem to get yourself out of bed before ten in the morning. It is going on eleven and your sister's bridal luncheon is in a little over an hour. Obviously you forgot but for some reason your sister wants you to be there, so I expect you to be there. For appearances sake." My adoptive mother nagged through the answering machine. She couldn't leave the message without slipping that last dig in, reminding me not only about the luncheon but that she didn't really want me there.

Unfortunately for her I had gotten a lot of press after helping SPTF solve the Witch murders. Her bridge club knew I was living in Salem now. She couldn't keep up the charade that I had moved to the West Coast and was far too busy working to make it back home for a visit. It hadn't been hard for me to avoid her and the Boston socialite scene. Until now that is. Still, my mother would probably give up her best diamonds before letting her snobby friends know the truth about her feelings for me, which bordered on hate.

I was definitely the black sheep growing up but it wasn't until last month I really understood why. That's when Arawn told me the truth. He was my real father and my real mother used the last of her magic and life to hide me from the war in Elysium with my adoptive parents. Knowing the truth about where I came from explained a lot but didn't excuse the ostracism that was my formative years. Don't get me wrong, I didn't live in a cupboard under the stairs or anything. My adoptive parents kept me clothed and fed, everything that was expected except love and compassion. Once they realized I wasn't like them and never would be, no matter how many Norm activities they forced me to participate in, I was pretty much an outcast. Things only got worse when they got pregnant with my sister. I left at seventeen and never looked back.

A couple years ago my sister looked me up. She was the collateral damage of my teenage years. It hurt to leave her behind. Francesca was the one person growing up that was always nice to me but I couldn't stay one minute longer in that house, not even for her. I think Frankie understood that. Just like I understood her not getting in touch with me until after she went off to college. I'd actually gone down to RISD to visit her a couple of times. When she told me she was engaged I secretly hoped it was to a starving artist and that she'd run off to Vegas to elope- causing a scandal in my mother's eyes and saving me an invitation to a big wedding. It wasn't of course. In Francesca's case pedigree won out. She was engaged to a charming young man finishing his law degree at Harvard and was having the wedding our mother had basically been planning since the doctor smacked Frankie's ass in the delivery room.

I completely forgot about the bridal luncheon and the rehearsal dinner later in the evening. In fact I forgot the wedding altogether.

"Shit." I said to Conry. "What do people wear to bridal luncheons anyway?"

He just stared at me as I headed back to my closet, grumbling the entire way. I hopped in the shower but skipped washing my hair. There was no way I'd get it washed and dried and still make it to the stupid lunch. I stood in front of my bed staring at the three outfits I laid out unable to decide what was most appropriate for lunch at my estranged parents. A simple skirt and blouse combo won out. I would have preferred the fitted plum colored cashmere sweater but the high collar of my blouse would hide the brand on my neck. No need to give my mother another reminder of what I was or more importantly to her what I wasn't. I pulled my hair back in a low bun and slipped on my heels.

If I traveled through the between I could skip traffic and still arrive at the luncheon fashionably late.

***

Using my new abilities in place of my car probably wasn't what Arawn had in mind when he showed me how to do this I thought as I mentally deconstructed my apartment and visualized my childhood home in Beacon Hill. The federal style row home came into view bustling with people. I managed to move through the cluster of people lingering by the front door only to be accosted by the caterer.

"Don't just stand there empty handed. Go get a tray and offer hors d' vours to the guests." The woman, who I could only assume was the chef by the white coat she stuffed herself into barked at me. Before I could object and inform her that I was a guest I was pushed into the kitchen. I opened my mouth to protest but was quickly informed I was not being paid to talk to her or to the guests. She shoved a large silver tray loaded with stuffed mushroom caps into my hands, spun me around and pushed me out into the room full of Boston's elite. I realized too late that I was on a collision course with my mother.

"Mushroom?" I asked one of the women talking with my mother. "You just have to try one."

I was probably the only one who noticed the flash of anger in my mother's eyes. Before anyone could so much as reach for one of the mushrooms she was snapping her fingers at one of the other waiters and pointing at my tray. A mortified young man hurried over to relieve me of the appetizers.

"Maurin this is Joanne Barton. We volunteer together at the hospital." My mother said forcing a smile.

"I didn't even know Kate had another daughter until I heard about your exploits on the news. It's amazing how you were able to overcome your condition and assist the police." Joanne extended her hand.

My condition? Were they saying I had some kind of disease on the news? Oh wait, she just meant being an Other. I hadn't been home in so long I forgot my mother's friends were almost as bad her. I reached out to shake Joanne's hand but my mother was moving before I made contact.

"Maurin, Francesca's been waiting for you to arrive. Why don't we go find your sister. If you'll excuse us a moment Joanne." My mother was practically dragging me away.

Old habits die hard. I didn't bother to pull away, nor did I bother to tell her I could shield. She wouldn't have tolerated either and we would just end up having another one of our famous arguments ruining Frankie's day. I hadn't been home half an hour but it was like I never left. I could feel my mother's embarrassment and irritation. Her disdain radiated off her skin like rays from the sun. If I stood next to her for too long I was bound to get burned.

"Honestly Maurin, you show up late, dressed like a waitress, could you at least pretend you belong here? For your sister's sake. And for the love of God don't touch anybody. It's bad enough your face was plastered all over the news, no one here needs to experience what you do first hand." She hissed through a porcelain smile.

I work for some of the most dangerous people in Massachusetts, I've faced Gods and demons but none of them compared to this woman. She could suck the life out of me faster than any vampire I knew. I looked down at my outfit. Crisp white blouse, black skirt. Ugh, no wonder the caterer shoved a tray in my hands. In my defense though, no waitress worth her salt would work a day in these heels. When I left my apartment I vowed today would be different. I would not be a victim of her cruel words and disapproval. I would not fall into the same patterns of insults and arguments. I would not revert back to the school girl desperate for the love and approval of a mother who would never give her either. I bit my cheek until I tasted blood to keep the rebellion burning in my chest from escaping.

By the time she had gotten to 'It's like you refused to control it. You wouldn't even try to be normal. I don't know why you couldn't have been more like your sister.' I was ready to go. I was trying to remember why I had subjected myself to an afternoon at home after almost a decade away when I caught sight of Francesca. Her auburn hair perfectly coiffed, her pleated skirt and sweater perfectly matched. In that Stepford Wives kind of way. She hardly looked like the inspired artist I saw in Providence last spring. Of course a lot had changed since then for both of us. Francesca turned up the dial on her million dollar smile, concentrating its full power on me. I felt a smile creep across my face despite the company at my side.

"Hey Frankie!" I said as my sister pulled me into a hug. I could feel my mother roll her eyes at the nickname. She always hated it when I called her that.

"You came." She whispered, surprise audible despite her hushed voice.

"I told you I would." I replied, not bothering to tell her how I had completely forgotten and if it wasn't for the viper masquerading as my mother I wouldn't have made it.

"I wouldn't have blamed you if you didn't." She said, starting to pull back from our embrace.

"Hmm, somehow I didn't get that impression when you were laying on the guilt trip, I mean inviting me to this." I teased.

She laughed and it was like someone ran their fingers through a wind chime. "Let me introduce you to some of my friends." She was born with a gravitational pull that seemed no one could escape. Not even me.

Chapter Two

After a couple of hours of pretending to be one of *the* Kincaides and not Maurin Kincaide I decided I had fulfilled my sisterly obligation. I was back in Salem, standing outside of The Daily Grind trying to muster the courage to go inside.

I hadn't spoken to Amalie since the Council stripped Mahalia and the coven of their council seat. Mahalia deserved everything the Council dished out and more for trying to kill me. I just wished it hadn't cost me my friendship with Amalie. And my favorite place to go for coffee. I wasn't officially banned but it was owned and operated by coven members. Somehow I doubted my money was good here. With a heavy heart I walked away from my favorite chair and the best croissants in Salem. A new coffee house had opened a couple of blocks away and I decided to give it a try.

Brewed Awakening. I stared at the sign hoping the coffee lived up to the name. The smell of freshly ground coffee hit my nose as soon as I walked through the door, so did the realization that coffee wasn't what I wanted. Brewed Awakening was nice enough. The coffee smelled heavenly and there were glass cases filled with fresh scones, muffins and even croissants. There were comfortable chairs and a couch nestled in between shelves loaded with used books. A book exchange sign hung above them. It was my kind of place. Except for one thing. This place was run by norms, which normally wouldn't have bothered me but after spending an afternoon at my mother's I'd had my fill for the day. I decided on something stronger. It's five o'clock some where I told myself and headed for Toil and Trouble where there was sure to be company more like me.

There was no need for a bouncer that early in the day so I just walked right in. It was still dark in the bar despite the early hour. Mike, the bartender, was behind the counter drying glasses. He looked up from the martini glass in his hands and nodded.

"You want the usual?" Mike asked, his eyes already back on the glass.

"Vodka. I'll take the bottle, sugar and lemons. "

"One of those days, huh?" He said as he set the bottle of Van Gogh and a shot glass on the counter.

"In the grand scheme of things I have definitely had worse but I just spent the afternoon with my mother, surrounded by women she wished I turned out to be. Trust me I earned a drink or two." I said, managing to grab a bowl of lemon wedges, bowl of sugar, the bottle and shot glass.

I had my choice of seats since the place was practically empty but found myself headed towards a booth in the back. I slid across the vinyl seat, pressed my back against the wall and stretched my legs out on the rectangular cushion. I undid the bun holding my hair, kicked off my heels, coated a lemon wedge in sugar and poured myself a shot. It took a lot more vodka to get drunk than it used to thanks to my metabolism. I was down to one third of the ingredients for lemon drop shooters before I started feeling the effects. This was going to be an expensive bender I thought as I tossed back another shot. I wasn't one for wallowing in self pity or trying to find solutions at the bottom of a bottle but halfway through- sitting across from the table where all my problems with the coven began- both seemed like good ideas. The spins finally threatened to take hold so I rested my head against the wall and closed my eyes.

I must have dozed off for a few minutes. Someone's fingers were tapping on the old wooden table. I opened one eye expecting Mike with the check but through the fog in my head I made out Cash's face. Maybe my nap was longer than a few minutes. I hoped I hadn't snored.

"I thought maybe you turned your phone off or something but I can see now you just decided to completely check out for awhile." Cash said, lifting the bottle to see how much was actually left. "What's up?"

"Fighting demons." I forced myself to sit up straight. Cash raised a brow at the mention of demons. "Not that kind." I grumbled, wishing it was a monster with gnashing teeth and glowing eyes that had me feeling this way. Actually that description fit my mother on more than one occasion.

"I was at my mother's, a luncheon for my sister. Her wedding is tomorrow." I explained.

Mike brought a coffee and set it down in front of Cash who pushed it over to me.

"Don't feel bad just because your younger sister is getting married before you." He laughed. "I'm sure the fanged freak is just waiting for the right moment."

I kicked him under the table connecting with his shin. I forgot I took my shoes off. I didn't hurt him, all I managed to do was jam my toe.

"Do I look like the kind of girl who obsesses about being engaged and planning a wedding? Don't answer that." I laughed when he started to smirk. I could only imagine what kind of girl he thought I actually looked like. "I have managed to avoid my family for almost ten years, going back home has me a little unnerved."

"Not a happy home coming I take it." He said nudging the coffee closer in the hopes that I would actually drink it.

"I didn't expect it to be. I'm just having a pity party, which you are crashing. So what's so important that you had to track me down instead of just harassing me when I got home per usual?" I slurred.

"I told you the challenge for Alpha is tonight." He said, as if that explained why he was sitting across from me.

"It's about time. But I don't see what pack business has to do with me. This is between you and Roul." I finally took a sip of the coffee, also known as battery acid. It was cold, strong and burnt.

"And you have to be there." He explained.

"Sorry, no can do. I've got another fun filled family evening ahead of me, the rehearsal dinner. Followed by the wedding tomorrow. So as you can see my dance card is full for the weekend." I told him, while wishing I could cancel my plans.

"So you'd rather hang out with the family that hates you? You a glutton for punishment or something?" Cash asked genuinely confused.

"I never said I'd rather be there but I already told my sister I would be." I tried to explain but I could tell he didn't get it. Packs didn't work like that. You were either a part of the pack or you weren't.

"Well you're just going to have to tell her you can't go." He caught me eyeing the bottle again and moved the vodka out of my reach. "You're in no condition to go anywhere in my opinion but you can't shirk your responsibilities to the Council."

I stuck my tongue out at him. We both knew I would be fine after an hour or so. "What responsibility?"

He sighed. "Doesn't anyone tell you anything?"

"That's what I keep saying!" I pounded my fist on the table, sloshing coffee over the rim of the cup. Mike's head popped up from under the bar where he had been switching out a keg at the sound of my fist connecting with the old wood table. He was watching us now, looking for signs of trouble. 'No trouble here', I thought and quickly grabbed a napkin out of the metal holder to clean up my mess.

Cash continued as I finished the rest of the cold coffee. "You're the liaison. That means you witness the challenge."

"I don't think that's what it means. In fact I'm pretty sure it doesn't. I'm the first liaison, they made up this damn position for me. Challenges have been going on for as longs as there have been werewolves, long before I came into the picture. Who witnessed them before?" I had a sneaking suspicion I wouldn't like his answer.

"She's tied up at the moment. Literally." He said.

I grimaced. "Mahalia."

"Since you're the reason she's spending time spindling spells for the fae, the task falls to you." He explained.

"She's the reason she's there, not me. She's in their prison for trying to kill me, remember? " I said indignantly.

"Like I said, you're the reason. Seriously Maurin, you know where you'd rather be. Why are we even having this conversation?" Cash knew I didn't want to go to any more of my family functions.

"You haven't met my mother." I said flatly.

"Neither have you." He said and I winced. "Sorry, that was uncalled for."

"No, you're right. I don't owe her anything. I wasn't going for her. Why do I let that woman do this to me? I don't belong there anyway." I mumbled that last part.

"Not your world, kid. You fit in just fine with us. Look if your sister is half as concerned with your feelings as you are with hers she'll understand." Cash was trying to be sympathetic but I could tell his patience was growing thin.

"How come you're here? Why didn't they send somebody else?" I asked suddenly realizing he didn't have time for this crap. He was supposed to be getting ready for the challenge.

"That's what I said." It was his turn to slam a fist on the table. "Olwyn insisted I was the only one you'd listen to with the bloodsucker gone."

Mike was watching us again. We were going to get tossed out if we kept smashing his table. I waived him off and looked at Cash. He'd saved my ass getting me off Winter Island. And Matthison's. I owed him.

"She was right." I muttered, digging in my purse for my phone. Cash signaled for Mike to bring us the check as I scrolled through my contacts for Frankie's number.

She picked up on the third ring. "Maurin, where'd you run off to? Never mind it doesn't matter. If you hurry up and get back home you can ride with us to the rehearsal."

Sometimes I wonder if we grew up in the same house. "Uh Frankie, about the rehearsal," I hesitated.

"You're not coming are you?" She asked over my mother's confirmations in the background. I could hear her I told you so's through the phone.

"I got called into work. I'm sorry, I'll make it up to you. Promise." I sighed, remembering all the times I told her that growing up whenever I bailed on some family obligation she was stuck going to because she really was their family.

"You can try, at the wedding tomorrow." She said, the windchimes were back in her voice as she said goodbye and hung up.

"Why didn't you just tell her the truth?"

"Are you serious? Sorry Frankie, I can't make it tonight because I have to go watch two werewolves try to kill each other over leadership of the Salem pack- because that would have gone over well. Besides, I didn't lie. Technically I am working."

"Whatever. Can we go now?" Cash left a stack of money on the table, more than enough to cover my tab, and slid out of the booth.

I slipped my shoes on and took his hand, letting him pull me across the seat and help me up. "Do I have time to go home and change?"

"I had hoped to talk you out of your clothes someday not help pick them out." He laughed.

I just rolled my eyes, grabbed his hand again and popped us back to my apartment.

***

We landed in my living room. I was getting better at moving through the between. The landing was a little bumpy probably because of the vodka but I didn't have to exert as much energy when I brought someone with me. Aidan made me practice over and over again, much to Arawn's delight. But I knew Aidan hadn't insisted on the training sessions to win favor with my father. He would never admit it but I knew he was terrified I would get stuck in the between where he couldn't reach me. He wanted me to be able to move through the between as easily as I breathed.

Cash's knees threatened to give out the second his feet hit the worn out carpet. "Don't ever do that again." He growled.

"Aww, what's the matter? Big bad wolf can't take a little jump through the between?" I mocked.

He just glowered at me, leaning on my couch for support. "Five minutes." I said, heading to my room.

For the second time today I wondered what to wear. My closet was divided into two categories. Things I wear to work -as in my old job- and everything else. SPTF had a dress code for detectives, which applied to me as well. The clothes I wore there were nice but not really me. At least I hadn't had to buy something to wear today- too bad I picked the one outfit that made me look like *the help*, I laughed in spite of myself. Seeing my mother's face while I was holding that tray had been worth it.

Deciding on jeans and a Bad Religion t-shirt layered over top of a snug long sleeve grey shirt, I put on a pair of wool socks and laced up my combat boots. I ran my fingers through my hair and caught my reflection in the mirror hanging over my dresser. I felt a little more like myself again. Cash was right. I fit in with them just fine. I pulled my hair up high in a messy bun and called out that I was ready.

Cash was waiting impatiently in the hallway. I practically knocked him over as I came out of my room.

"About damn time." He grumbled. I slid past him, opening the hall closet to get my leather jacket.

I felt his fingers graze my neck and I flinched. Aidan's jealousy, his comment about not doubting Cash dreamed about me flashed in my mind. Suddenly Cash's teasing didn't seem so innocent any more. "What the hell Cash?"

"When did you get that?" He asked.

"What?" I had no idea what he was talking about.

"That." He said, poking my neck. Relief swam through me when I realized his touch hadn't been anything more than curiosity.

I ran into the bathroom, positioning the medicine cabinet just right so I could see the back of my neck in the mirror. What the?

"Cool ink, I don't remember seeing it on Winter Island. Who's your artist?" Cash asked.

I didn't answer. I was too busy pulling at the collar of my shirts to see how far it went down my spine. I was wearing a tank top and boy shorts last night and he hadn't noticed. Although knowing Cash he was paying more attention to my ass than my back, plus my hair was down. The Celtic knots wove their way down three vertebrae at least. I staggered out of the bathroom and yanked my layered shirts over my head, clinging them to my chest. "How far down does it go?"

Cash's eyes widened. "Does your vampire know about this deep dark desire you have to take your clothes off in front of me?" He dragged his palm down his face, tugging a little on his goatee. A small growl rumbled in his chest. "I can't believe I'm saying this, that reality trip thing you do must have done something to my brain. Put your clothes back on Maurin." He was laughing.

I stomped my foot, pissed. "How far Cash?" I was tired of his joking around. I had been marked again and this time I had no idea how it happened.

"Like half way down your back but it kind of fades out as it goes. Pretty cool effect." He said, his eyes raking over my exposed upper body.

"It's not an effect. It's not even supposed to be there." I pushed past the anger and tried to think.

"Damn it, Arawn!" I shouted, even though I didn't think he could hear me cursing his name. I pulled my shirts back over my head and forced my arms through the sleeves, not caring if he caught a glimpse of my bra.

Cash didn't know it yet but we were taking a little detour on our way to the challenge. I grabbed his hand before he realized what I was doing and could pull away. My one bedroom apartment slipped from my sight, quickly replaced with the familiar grounds outside of the vampire keep.

Gallows Hill park. Arawn had told me that if I came through the between here he would know. I was counting on it. I stood my ground, waiting to ask my father why I suddenly had a tattoo running down my spine.

"I thought I told you not to do that anymore!" Cash roared.

"Oh quit complaining. It's not that bad. Aidan does it all the time. Are you saying there's something he can do that you can't?" I don't know why I was rattling his cage.

"It pulls my wolf closer to the surface. I almost shifted this time." His voice was rough.

"Sorry, I didn't know." I admitted.

"Well now you do, so don't do it again." He stiffened at my expression. "What?"

"We'll have to travel in the between one more time tonight if you want to make it to the challenge." I mumbled.

"If I lose because of you I will come back and haunt the shit out of you. I will make your bedroom my permanent ghostly residence." He may have been making a joke but the seriousness of the situation suddenly hit me.

The challenge was to the death. Even if he yielded, not that Cash ever would, Roul was within his rights to kill him. It was a good possibility Cash would be dead by the end of the night. I struggled for a moment with the feelings that seemed to stir up. I was about to erase the awkwardness I felt with a joke about how Aidan would probably have something to say about him spending his afterlife in my apartment.

Before I could reply my father appeared. "Maurin. I didn't expect to see you tonight."

"Arawn." He tilted his head, looking at me sideways. "Father." I ground out.

"You wish to speak with me?" He asked, his eyes flitting around taking everything in. "I see you brought one dog with you, but not the one I assigned. Where is Conry?"

I didn't say anything. I forgot to bring him with me. Again. I couldn't take him to the luncheon, even Arawn would give me that, but here I was heading off on another Council task and had left my guardian at home. A growl formed at the back of Cash's throat over the dog comment. I shook my head.

"I was a little distracted by the Celtic knots running down my spine." I told him.

"You will have to do better than that daughter. Life is full of distractions. That is why I gave him to you. So that there was always someone at your back." With a wave of his hand reality parted and Conry slipped through the between. I could almost see my apartment behind him.

Conry came to stand beside me and my nerves instantly calmed. I gave him a couple scratches behind his ears and a pat on his massive side. "Good boy." I whispered and brought my attention back to my father.

"May I see the marks?" He asked as if it was no big deal. I turned around, tugging at the collar again. "The between is accepting you. This is wonderful."

"The between is accepting me?" I asked, totally confused. "You make it sound like a sorority or something."

"No, but it is a force. It is magic that allows you to move through the place between realities. It has been getting easier hasn't it?" He said, referring to my practice sessions with Aidan.

"Yes." I hadn't even broken a sweat moving with Cash tonight and he resisted pretty hard the second time.

"The magic has marked you. Think of it as a tuning fork, resonating your body to the right pitch to move through the between without having to breakdown reality." He explained.

"That's how you do it. That first night, you moved three of us with you through the between like a hot knife through butter." I said.

Rather than say anything he pushed up the sleeves of his sapphire tunic exposing a helix of Celtic knots running up his arm. "It's the same design as mine." I gasped.

"More proof you are my daughter." He moved closer.

Cash cleared his throat loudly, looking at his watch. "This is all really touching, but I've got some where I'm supposed to be."

Arawn's expression darkened and his grip tightened around the hilt of the short sword fastened to his leather belt. He shook his head to clear away the anger. "You would do well to remember your place wolf. You are not an Alpha yet. Daughter, we will continue this conversation another time." And just like that he was gone.

"Cash, you need to watch yourself around him. He's not bound by Council law." I warned.

"That guy likes to hear himself talk. I don't have all night." Cash snapped.

"We've got plenty of time. I can have us at the challenge in sixty seconds." I said confidently.

"No you can't. I told you I wasn't doing that again. We'll go borrow one of Agrona's cars." He crossed his arms stubbornly over his chest.

"Quit being such a baby. If I don't have to focus so hard on breaking down reality I can concentrate more on keeping it from bothering you." I told him. "Now, where are we going?"

"Winter Island."

Of course, why would it be anywhere else?

Chapter Three

I brought us to the spot on Winter Island where Cash had found me contemplating a swim through the bitter Atlantic to a small boat anchored just off shore in a last ditch effort to get Matthison and myself off the island. I shivered both from the cold and memories of what had happened here. Cash moved closer and I soaked up the warmth from his hot blooded nature coming off of him in waves. Conry was facing the old hanger, ears pricked up, twitching as he listened for something or someone. A growl soft at first began to rumble up from his chest. It was the first time since Arawn gave him to me that he truly tried to warn me. His growl vibrated through my bones, making my teeth chatter. I spun around, pushing past Cash as my guardian sounded off a warning. I was expecting to see that death itself had finally come to claim me. I wouldn't have been surprised. I had evaded it too many times already.

I couldn't reconcile what was right in front of me with what Conry was trying to tell me. Olwyn? Why was Conry reacting to her this way? Maybe he was picking up on her feelings toward Cash and we were just getting caught in the crossfire. Olwyn was throwing some serious hate Cash's way and I just happened to be standing in front of him.

"It's okay Conry, it's okay boy." I stroked his back, trying to reassure him Olwyn was our friend.

"Maurin, if I didn't know better I would say you were sleeping with the enemy. You're not slipping

him any pack secrets over pillow talk I hope."
Olwyn was eyeing Cash, still behind me in a
protective stance.

"I don't know any pack secrets and not that it's
any of your business but the only one keeping my
bed warm is my dog." I said wondering where this
was going.

"That's because vampires are cold blooded
dear. Pity you let Agrona get her fangs into you so
easily. How do you do it? Spending time with a wolf
during the day and a vampire at night? I hope
exhaustion won't impede your ability to do your
duty tonight." There was anger in her voice.

I knew it didn't have anything to do with
vampires or Cash. Well maybe that had a little to
do with it. She was close to Mahalia though and I
had a sneaking suspicion she blamed me for
Mahalia's incarceration with the Fae. That was
what Conry was picking up on. Funny how Olwyn
seemed to forget the part where Mahalia tried to
kill me.

"Nobody has their fangs in me." I shot back
suddenly on the defensive. "And I wouldn't call
banging on Cash's door every morning at three
o'clock yelling at him to turn his TV down spending
time together. Of course if Roul was so concerned
about Cash moving into my apartment building he
should have held the challenge a couple weeks
ago."

Olwyn didn't say anything else, instead she
gave me a look that said you don't belong here.
Yup, she was somehow holding me responsible for

Mahalia's punishment. Well bring it on bitch, I thought. I spent a lifetime on the receiving end of looks like that. I wasn't planning on backing down. The Council expected me to witness the challenge and I was going to do just that. Screw her and her misplaced anger. She should have been pissed her best friend turned out to be a lying, murderous bitch.

We followed her into the old hanger and I was immediately assaulted with memories. I could practically smell the blood that still stained the concrete floor. Mine, Matthison's and the Butcher's. 'You said I could keep her. She likes to play my games.' I could hear the Butcher's voice in my head. I thought I scrubbed those words from my mind like I had scrubbed his blood from my body. My hand was on my mid section, splayed across the spot where he would have carved another message to the Coven before I snapped myself out of it. I had killed the Butcher. It seemed that despite having healed the cuts and bruises the Butcher's blocky hands had inflicted on my body, my mind had not done the same.

Olwyn was watching me with satisfaction. I assumed she had selected the location and it had had the desired effect. She stood across from me, elegant even in her casual attire of jeans, riding boots and perfectly tailored cream leather jacket, with a look of mock innocence.

I shoved the memory of the Butcher from my mind and tried to focus. What had changed since the first night I met her at Baylen's? I had aligned myself with her and her husband, done everything they asked leading up to tonight -including blowing off my sister- and she wanted to play mind games? Perhaps I had chosen the wrong side. After all, it was Cash that had found me when I was branded and beaten beyond recognition. When my friend's life was hanging by a thread it was Cash who got him to the hospital. He stuck with me at Mahalia's when I confronted Oberon and has never asked for anything in return. I sucked in a breath when it dawned on me. Somewhere along the way Cash and I had become friends. And everyone here knew it. Now Olwyn had two reasons not to like me.

There wasn't a friendly face in the crowd surrounding Roul for Cash or myself. Conry's hackles were up as the snarls got louder with our approach. I kept my hand on his back in an effort to comfort the both of us. We were at the edge of the pack's circle and I could feel their collective growl hum through my body. I looked across the "ring" at Roul. There was a look of betrayal on his face. I shrugged my shoulders, as if to say this is your fault. You're the one who practically glued him to my ass. He surprised me with a nod that seemed to say I know.

Tybalt stepped forward and let out a growl that commanded everyone's attention. Apparently he was playing the role of master of ceremonies tonight. "The challenger will step forward."

Cash shrugged out of his black Carhardt jacket, dropping it at my feet before walking to the center of the room. He rolled his shoulders a few times and cracked his neck. Muscles rippled beneath his shirt and for the first time I saw just how much strength he kept caged inside. I had caught a glimpse of the Alpha he could become in the helicopter a few weeks ago when he saw the brand on my neck. Anger rolled off him in waves that night, enough to have every wolf in the chopper with us on the verge of shifting. Still, I had under estimated him, distracted by his arrogance and smart ass comments. No wonder Roul had been putting this off.

Tybalt's booming voice filled the room again when he called the Alpha forward. Roul met Cash in the center of the makeshift ring. They stood there toe to toe facing off like boxers in a championship fight with Tybalt in between them as referee. He stepped back to the edge of the ring signaling the battle for Alpha had begun. The opponents circled each other cautiously at first. Roul swung with a right. Cash easily dodged it. Suddenly they were on each other in a blur of fists. It was hard to tell who was winning. When one of them seemed to be gaining ground the other rallied.

Blood and sweat flew as Roul and Cash each landed blows. The scales seemed to tip in the reigning Alpha's favor when Roul slashed Cash's stomach in a move I hadn't known was possible. Roul had partially shifted, arming himself with the massive paws and deadly claws of his wolf. My heart was suddenly in my throat. Could Cash shift his hands too? I didn't think shifting completely into his wolf would help him against the half wolf fighting him.

Blood soaked the front of Cash's shirt. Roul had shifted his face. His sneer made more terrifying by powerful jaws and deadly canines as he pressed his advantage. Cash swung with a shifted hand, connecting his paw with the side of Roul's face. Cash's claws sliced through Roul's left eye and cheek. I stifled a cheer as I caught sight of Olwyn. Terror flashed across her face as she realized for the first time how close she was to losing her mate. They were hoping Roul's ability to partially shift would give him the upper hand in the fight. I knew from the fear in her eyes that they hadn't known Cash could as well. Was that something only an Alpha was supposed to be able to do? I was suddenly hyper aware of how little I actually knew about the wolves. I wouldn't get an answer to the questions swirling around in my mind until the challenge was over. The sound of snapping jaws brought my attention back to the fight.

Two fully shifted massive wolves circled each other in the ring. It occurred to me that I had never seen Cash shift. I had fought with him against a demon horde but it was always a man at my side. If he had shifted during the battle I hadn't been there to see it. The murmurs from the crowd said I wasn't the only one who had never see Cash shift. I hadn't expected a timber wolf. While they were evenly matched as men, Cash was easily twice the size of Roul as a wolf.

Black fur momentarily blocked my view as Roul pounced on his opponent. Snarling jaws snapped and tore into flesh and fur as the two wolves tried to kill each other. Cash clamped down on Roul's front right leg. Blood welled up, seeping out the side of Cash's jaws. Roul bit down hard on the scruff of Cash's neck staining his fur red. There was the distinct sound of breaking bones. Roul whimpered and released his grip on the back of Cash's neck, limping back toward the edge of the circle. Cash stalked forward. Thinking he had Roul on the ropes he moved in for the kill. He pushed off of his hind legs, lunging forward but in his rush to finish the Alpha he made a novice mistake. I couldn't help the gasp that escaped my mouth as soon as I saw it.

Roul waited until the last possible second. Just as Cash was about to take him down, he caught the exposed neck of his challenger in his vice like jaws. He wrestled Cash to his back, never loosening his grip on his neck. Cash shifted back, vulnerable as a man, naked and covered in blood beneath a wolf. I fought the urge to call the fight. I shuffled my feet, ready to jump in between them and put an end to it. This was insane, no one had to die.

Tybalt laid a heavy hand on my shoulder, squeezing harder than necessary. "Don't even think about it. The penalty for interfering in a challenge is death. Just to clarify, that applies to the Council Liaison." I tried to shake him off but he wasn't letting me go.

Roul's paws were on Cash's chest, pressing him into the concrete as he crushed his windpipe. Cash struggled to get out from under the huge wolf. Roul sensed the end was near and clamped down tighter. I didn't want to watch this. If someone told me twenty four hours ago I would mourn the loss of Cash I would have laughed in their face. Now that the moment was here I struggled with the emotions that swelled in my chest. Eyes closed, I dropped my head. I couldn't bear to watch him die.

Small but powerful fingers grabbed my chin hard enough to bruise and forced my head up. "Open your eyes." Olwyn demanded. I met her cold eyes with a steely gaze of my own, gaining confidence from Conry's growls. She jerked my head to the side, bringing the fight back into full view. I kept a hand on my guardian to make sure he didn't break any pack rules. I had a feeling Olwyn was trying to push one of us over the edge. She was so confident in her husband's victory she never took her eyes off me. Conry never took his eyes off her.

Cash had a hand on both of Roul's jaw. He managed to wedge his fingers between his neck and Roul's teeth. His eyes met mine. My brain struggled to process the confidence I saw on his face. Didn't he know he was losing? What the? Was that a wink? Cash's lips curved up in a half smile as he took in my confusion. Without ever breaking eye contact he began to force Roul's jaws apart. Blood flowed freely from the puncture wounds in his neck. Cash's biceps flexed as he unleashed the power coiled inside them. It cost Roul more energy than he could afford to hold Cash in that position for so long. Roul couldn't finish him off and Cash knew it. With a swift jerk Cash ripped Roul's jaws apart. Cash slipped an arm around Roul's neck and wrapped his other hand around the muzzle. Roul's bottom jaw flapped around unsupported as Cash snapped his neck. He pushed Roul's body off to the side and got up. He stood over the dead Alpha and howled.

With shaking hands Olwyn released her grip on my face. She watched in shock as her pack knelt to recognize their new Alpha. Their new Alpha! Her husband was dead. Tremors racked her body and I felt her shift before I saw it. There was shouting. People yelling grab her, stop her. She was airborne and headed straight for Cash, snarling ferociously. She was all beast, the woman in her died with her mate. Anticipating this would happen Cash was ready for her. Just before she landed on him he connected a backhand that sent her soaring across the room. The blow would have killed a mortal woman but Olwyn didn't stay down for long. After collapsing on her first attempt to stand, she found her second wind. Fueled by the insanity losing one's mate obviously caused she lunged again. Cash thwarted her attack just as easily the second time.

Before I had the chance to wonder why no one was making a serious effort to stop her I was crushed beneath the massive weight of her wolf. I was struggling to push her off me, trying desperately to keep her from clamping down with her long canines and puncturing my flesh. I didn't know if I could be turned but I had no desire to find out. When I was attacked by the Afrit I hadn't been able to stop poison from spreading through my body alone. Would I have the same kind of reaction to a wolf bite? Aidan wasn't back from Iceland yet and I was pretty sure I wouldn't be getting any Alicorn from the Coven. I needed to keep her teeth away from my body but I could feel her cold, wet nose press against mine. Damn, she weighed more as a wolf than I would have imagined. I screamed her name in an effort to call the woman I knew forward but there was no recognition in the wild eyes of her wolf. I called for Conry. Where was he? I hammered fist after fist into her ribs with my right hand all the while keeping my left forearm crushed against her throat. She yelped and I knew my guardian had a hold of her. Hot, stank wolf breath assaulted me. She was still too close. Conry's teeth dug into her hind leg. He managed to drag her off of me enough for me to jam my fingers into her eye. She finally reared back. Without the combined weight of Olwyn and Conry pressing me into the concrete I was finally able to buck her off. Conry never let go of her hind quarter, dragging her further away. I scrambled to my feet, instinctively reaching for my sword. I knew I would have to kill her to stop her. She was too far gone for there to be any other outcome.

My fingers closed around air instead of the hilt of my sword. Shit. In my haste to talk to Arawn I had left more than just Conry at home. If Arawn had noticed he'd failed to bring the Retaliator through the between with Conry. I could have done without the lesson he was apparently trying to teach me. I honestly hadn't given my sword much thought before seeing as how I was supposed to be among friends. A mistake I wouldn't make again.

"Cash, a little help would be nice!" I yelled. A grunt was his only response. I decided it was worth the risk to take my eyes off Olwyn long enough to see what was happening with Cash. While I had been busy fighting off Olwyn, Cash had gotten caught up in a fight of his own. It seemed some of the pack refused to acknowledge him as their Alpha and remained loyal to Roul.

Unlike the perfectly choreographed fight scenes in movies, they didn't jump him one at a time. He went down swinging under the weight of all four wolves. A Timber wolf erupted from beneath the mass of fur and deadly teeth that had been attacking him. He had already evened the odds to two against one when I brought my attention back to Olwyn.

Conry still had her trapped in his jaws. She rolled onto her side and clamped down the side of his head. Olwyn's wolf was stronger without the woman to keep her in check. She managed to bite down hard enough to cause Conry to loosen his grip for a second. A second was all she needed. She rocketed up from beneath him. Her paws found purchase and she barreled into my shins. My back made contact with the hard concrete floor a half second before my head did. She was on top of me again. I couldn't breathe, from having the wind knocked out of me and Olwyn standing on my chest. Conry had a hold of her again and proceeded to drag her off me. Her claws dug in, shredding my clothes and stomach. My flesh felt like it was on fire where her sharp nails had torn threw it and I screamed. The searing pain spread across my stomach and up my chest. My heart rate picked up until I thought it was going to explode. I couldn't keep the screams in as the pain racked my body.

Conry managed to get on top of her. She fought beneath him as he tore through her dense coat, ripping meat from bone. I forced myself to get up. My body was barely cooperating but somehow I had to finish this. Conry finally released her. Olwyn lay whimpering in a bloody heap at my feet.

"Put the bitch out of her misery." Cash placed a gun in my hand.

"You're the alpha, why don't..." The look Cash gave me stopped me from finishing the question. He was alpha now and I was not going to give him shit in front of the pack.

My arms trembled from the effort it took to stay standing and hold the brushed steel .50 cal ae Desert Eagle out in front of me. I didn't know if I could handle the recoil in my current state. I took a deep breath to find my center and steady my hands.

"She could be like this for days before she died. Her mate is dead, she let her wolf consume her. She'll never be the same again." Cash had mistaken the shakes caused by the fever burning me up from the inside out as hesitation to kill Olwyn. I couldn't afford to waste any energy in correcting him.

My palms, like every other part of my body had broken out in a cold sweat. I alternated rubbing my hands down the front of my jeans then returned to a stance perfected over three years of required range time while working for SPTF. I wasn't holding the Retaliator but the result would be the same. This gun could take down a bear shifter with no problem. Just like my sword, there was no healing from the mess the .50 cal would make. I looked down the sight. It shouldn't have been so hard to focus on the unusually large target. I could make this shot with my eyes closed from across the room but I couldn't seem to keep it lined up. I wasn't going to be able to stay upright much longer. Fuck it. With a bullet this big there was a little room for error, right? I didn't have to hit her forehead dead center. I took another deep breath, exhaled and pulled the trigger. The bullet hit Olwyn and then I hit the floor.

I didn't have control of my body any more. I succumbed to the seizures that had threatened to take hold before I pulled the trigger. Cash was shouting orders to his new pack as he dropped to his knees beside me. Waiting until the seizing subsided, he rolled me onto my back and tore off what was left of my shirt exposing the inflamed gouges that ran the length of my stomach from rib cage to the waistline of my low rise jeans. Cash gave a hard tug, forcing the button and zipper to give way. I was teetering on the edge of unconsciousness but I still managed to grab his wrist.

"If you don't let me heal you you'll turn." Cash growled.

"Don't. Know. That. For. Sure." I ground out.

"You want to take that chance? You couldn't stop the Afrit's poison from spreading. Now move your fucking hand or I'll have Tybalt restrain you. Will somebody get her dog out of here for fucks sake! I can't do anything with him hovering over her." Cash took a small jar from one of his wolves, while two more attempted to drag Conry away -

only managing to move him back enough for Cash to work and only because he let them.

I tried to focus on how interesting it was that Tybalt wasn't one of the wolves fighting Cash after he won the challenge and the pack instead of the pain. Tybalt had been Roulss second. If anyone was going to avenge the fallen alpha my money would have been on Tybalt. I lost my train of thought and damn near my mind as Cash spread some sort of salve over my wounds.

"Careful, too much of that shit and she'll die from the Wolfsbane." Tybalt warned.

"I'm not trying to kill her, just the possibility of her becoming a wolf." Cash snarled.

"Alpha, I'm not challenging, " Cash roared but Tybalt persisted. "She's not a were. You can't just kill her wolf with an over dose of Aconite like some rogue. You don't know for sure if she'll even change. Wolfsbane is deadly to humans. We could call in the Coven."

"Don't you think I know that? And we are not calling the Coven. Half of them tried to kill her last month. They'd probably give her Belladonna instead of Alicorn. I've used Wolfsbane before. It was my job to deal with the rogues and their victims in Boston. I've used it to separate wolf from man more times than I care to remember. I've done this before on a human. A small dose, applied immediately to the wound will kill the infection before it has a chance to take hold, like an antidote." Cash said, trying to calm his wolf and focus on me.

There were a million questions swirling around in my head. What did they mean separate a rogue from its wolf? They could do that? Kill someone's wolf? He'd done this to a human? But I'm not human. Before I had a chance to ask any of them I was overcome with pain. If I thought I was on fire before I was mistaken. That was just smoldering embers compared to this. My blood was suddenly molten lava. I pulled my knees up to my chest, rolled onto my side in the fetal position and instantly regretted it. Pain shot through my mid section, like someone was scrambling my intestines with red hot pokers. I kicked my legs back out and rolled over. My back arched as the pain racked through my stomach and my blood felt like it was boiling again. I was being cooked from the inside out. Something was wrong. The Wolfsbane wasn't working. I needed to tell Cash before the fever or whatever the hell this was fried my brain. The only thing that came out of my mouth when I tried to talk was a scream so I clamped my jaws shut.

"Hold her legs Tybalt. It'll pass Maurin. The burning will stop. You're doing great, you're going to be fine." Cash was holding my shoulders down, whispering encouragements in my ear like we were in a Lamaze class instead of laying on the concrete floor with hell fire burning my insides. Despite his best efforts to conceal it, I caught the faintest hint of uncertainty in his voice.

"Damn, she heals fast. You think enough of the Wolfsbane got into her blood stream before she knit back together?" Tybalt was just shaking his head, still in disbelief over how fast I had healed. He moved a hand off one of my legs to trace the freshly closed skin.

I knew it was scab free and the light pink fleshy color of new scar tissue. I may be able to heal fast but I still hadn't mastered it yet. Injuries this bad obviously weren't outside my abilities but what I had just done was the equivalent of a field dressing compared to what I should have been capable of. I was collecting scars like some people collected coins.

Thankfully Cash was right and the pain was sub siding. It no longer felt like my body was the same temperature as magma. It was easier to think now that I seemed to only suffer from severe flu like symptoms. I managed to talk through the nausea. "Don't touch me." My need to not have anyone touch my all too sensitive skin came out sounding more like repulsion at having Tybalt's hand on my stomach. I saw the flash of anger and hurt in his eyes. He had tried to help me, even after the only pack leaders he had ever known were killed. He immediately recognized Cash as alpha and followed his orders knowing full well as second in command to Roul the other wolves would look to him to follow or fight. I wanted to smooth things over but didn't have the energy for more than "Sorry, still hurts like a son of a bitch."

I forced myself up onto my elbows, grimacing as I felt the new scar tissue stretch. I looked down the length of my body sizing up the Freddie Krueger like slash marks on my otherwise flawless stomach. "Damn, there goes bikini season." I tried to make light of the situation.

"There's the Maurin Kincaide I know." Cash chuckled.

Tybalt yanked his tee shirt over his head and tossed it to me. I thanked him and pulled it on. He was easily a foot and a half taller than me and twice as wide so I was swimming in dark blue cotton but it sure beat sitting there in jeans and a bra.

Cash extended his hand and I took it, allowing him to pull me to my feet. Sensing the worst of my healing process was over Conry shook off the two wolves holding onto him and settled himself at my feet. I bent down, trying not to wince as the scars stretched again, and wrapped my arms around Conry's neck. I even let him lick my face a couple of times. Cash cleared his throat, breaking up our little reunion.

I gave him a sideways glance as I untangled myself from my dog. He gave a short, tight nod to his left. Evidence of the challenge that took place for the right to lead the Salem pack still littered the ground. Remnants of clothes shredded from shifting, tufts of fur and blood where everywhere. Just beyond Cash lay the bodies of Roul and Olwyn. If I hadn't been here for the whole brutal and bloody battle I doubt I wouldn't have recognized them as the former alpha and his mate. Roul's body was covered with bruises and claw marks. His eyes frozen in shock, reflecting the exact moment he realized he was about to die. His bottom jaw barely attached by a strap of skin on his neck rested on his chest. I swallowed hard, trying not to throw up. Olwyn was stretched out next to him. A hole the size of a Kennedy half dollar in her face where the apple of her right cheek would have been was the only evidence that I had shot her. Never having fired a Desert Eagle before I half expected to see her head blown clear off. Something told me the exit wound would be larger but I wasn't rolling her over to find out. Looking at their lifeless bodies I was surprised, or maybe it was disappointment, at how little I felt.

While I stood beside Cash struggling with my indifference, grief gripped the pack. Men and women -all of them wolves and now Cash's pack- filled the old military hanger to max capacity. All eyes were downcast in a show of submission and respect as they waited for their alpha to address them. Their pain and fear of the unknown was easy to read despite their averted eyes.

Cash's voice filled the vacuum. His first command as alpha caught me completely off guard. "Maurin is under pack protection, my protection. There will be no retribution for the death of the omega from an obvious act of self defense. Any wolf in violation of this will suffer my wrath, for a very long and painful time before succumbing to Wolfsbane. By my order she is free to leave and report back to the Council what she has witnessed tonight."

I took that as my cue to exit. I had seen more than enough of the inner workings of the pack for one night anyway. I wasn't sure it was wise to make his first order as alpha a threat but if he felt it was necessary I wasn't going to argue. Cash had accomplished two things in making that statement.

One, now I knew there was a very real possibility one or more of the pack could come after me. And two the pack knew he would not only cause bodily harm but rip the wolf from their body. A fate I assumed was worse than death since that hadn't even been an option.

Conry was right on my heels as I broke the veil that separated reality from the between and went home. I could still hear the gasps and whispers of how the hell did I just do that as the rip in reality closed and I collapsed on my couch.

Chapter Four

My phone was ringing incessantly. I had been trying to ignore it for the last hour. Ten rings ago I had decided it wasn't a solicitor and most likely another emergency but I couldn't bring myself to get up off the couch and answer it. Five rings ago it dawned on me it was most likely the woman I called my mother -since my cell phone hadn't rung once, simply because I never gave her the number- and I had even less motivation to pick up. Certain she was just calling to give me grief for letting Frankie down by choosing work over my sister I was determined to let the phone ring all night - well technically morning. One ring ago I realized what time it really was and that in lieu of leaving hateful messages on my machine she chose to hang up and dial again, I concluded something was actually wrong.

"Hello?" I never bothered to put the receiver next to my ear, the skeptical part of me ready to hang up at the first insult.

"I know you are behind this. You're always making a mess of everything. You're miserable and alone, no surprise there but I will not allow you to drag your sister down with you. Put Francesca on the phone now!" She was yelling, a show of passion and anger I had never seen before.

I was about to hit the off button on my phone when I read between the insults. My sister wasn't home. "Frankie's not here." I croaked, exhaustion still audible in my voice.

"Don't bother lying. I know she's there. Where else would she be?" She regained her composure and was back to the ice queen I was familiar with.

"I said she's not here. So she went out for awhile, that's not a crime. She's a grown woman. Give her some space." Why did I answer the phone?

"She was supposed to be here hours ago. You expect me to believe your sister just went out for a walk the morning of her wedding and lost track of time? The hair stylist and make-up artist are already here, the photographer is on his way and your sister just went for a stroll, is that it?" She barked.

"Don't bite my head off, I'm not the one who lost the bride. That was on your watch." I snapped back. "The way this conversation should have gone was Maurin your sister took off. She's not here or at her apartment. I don't know where else to look. I need your help."

I was met with silence on the other end. "I am hanging up now. Call me if she changes her mind about the whole runaway bride thing."

"You care more about breaking me than your sister? Fine Maurin, I need your help." The last part was laced with anger.

I knew how much it cost her to say those words. A smile crept across my face. I would have looked for Frankie anyway. "I'll bring her home."

She didn't say thank you or anything else for that matter before she hung up. I dragged myself off the couch, managing to get myself cleaned up in record time despite lingering aches and pains from last night's activities. I had planned on going to see the Council before the ceremony. If I didn't find Frankie fast there wouldn't be enough time and standing up the Council was not an option. Of course if I didn't find her there wouldn't be a ceremony to worry about so it wouldn't matter. That line of thinking wasn't getting me any closer to finding my sister. I gave a little whistle for Conry. I already knew where my first stop was going to be.

My soon to be brother-in-law was a mess sitting on their expensive leather couch in the clothes he had obviously slept in. Hang over, suffering from the same cold feet as my sister, concern for her safety or guilt for having done something to make her run? I intended to find out.

Moving through the between was definitely a stealthy mode of transportation. He never heard me come in. I had been watching him for a couple minutes and he had no clue I was there. Conry gave a little huff, announcing our presence.

I wasn't sure how much Michael actually knew about me but the look of absolute terror on his face told me not nearly enough. It was becoming painfully obvious that even Frankie wasn't comfortable telling people what I really was. Although in her defense, it wasn't like I told her exactly what that was.

"How the hell... Your sister said you were... but she never said you could... What are you?" Michael sputtered.

"All that Ivy League education and you can't even manage to string a proper sentence together. You disappoint me Michael." His face was stricken with fear. His chest heaved as he sucked in breath after breath trying to calm down and failing miserably. He was going to hyperventilate. "In her defense, she doesn't have a clue about what I really am. What did you do to my sister Michael?" I let the menace in my voice hang in the air before pressing him further.

"I asked you a question. What did you do to make my sister run Michael?" My voice was cold, void of all emotion. It had the desired effect.

"We, we had a fight. I..." He stammered.

I moved with a swiftness I wouldn't have thought possible given my lack of sleep and time to heal."If there is so much as a hair out of place when I find her..." I warned. I jerked him up off the couch. Conry sensed my anger and moved forward, snarling.

"I didn't touch her. I swear." He practically shrieked, trying to pry my grip from his no doubt expensive dress shirt. Sensing the effort to free himself was pointless he hung there defeated and completely emasculated.

"So why isn't she at her mother's putting her on wedding dress?" I gave him a little shake, letting him know I wasn't entirely convinced. His face showed his confusion over my Freudian slip, so I shook him again until I could see he was focused once again on my sister and not the state of my relationship with my family. He'd have to do better at hiding his emotion if he had any hope of being a lawyer.

"We were talking about the wedding, about moving to D.C. in the summer. My father said I shouldn't say anything, that what she didn't know wouldn't hurt her." He was a blubbering mess and hadn't even actually confessed yet. I could only imagine how this went with Frankie last night.

I knew my expression darkened as my grip tightened. "What did you do? Make it quick Michael, my patience is wearing thin."

"It was a few months before we were engaged. There was this study group for the bar, every Thursday. You know pizza and beer, that kind of thing." I waved him on with my free hand hoping he would get to the point so I could start looking for Frankie. "Ashley was struggling with the mock exam, at least she said she was. I stayed to help. I didn't mean for anything to happen. One minute we were going over constitutional law and the next we were.....I told Frankie it was meaningless. If anything it made me realize how much I loved her."

One thing led to another? His words gave a ring of truth the ridiculous fears I had earlier about Aidan and the mysterious woman he was traveling with. I was dangerously close to losing control of my temper.

"I'm sure she took comfort in the fact that the sex was meaningless. You're a complete fucking idiot. You waited until the night before your wedding to confess your inability to keep your dick in your pants?" I dropped him on the couch with enough force to rock it backwards. The back of his head smacked the wall hard enough to dent the drywall. I watched with satisfaction as his eyes rolled back and his eyelids fluttered. From the looks of the apartment Frankie left before she had time to got angry. Giving him a mild concussion was the least I could do.

I was already slipping into the between when he regained his ability to focus. He was begging me to tell her how sorry he was and convince her to come home as their apartment disappeared. I stood in the place between realities and tried to figure out my next move. It wasn't like I'd spent a lot of time hanging out with my sister lately. I didn't have a clue where she went when she needed to be alone.

"Where do you think she is Conry? How are we going to find her, huh boy?" I said squatting down to give him a good scratch behind his ears. He nudged me with his muzzle and knocked me off balance. I plopped down beside him. "We don't have time to play Conry. We need to find Frankie and get her to at least call home. Maybe she took the train to Providence."

This was the longest I had been in the between with no clear destination. It was like lucid dreaming. Places I had used the between to travel to flashed in front of me. I would think of a place Frankie might be and it would begin to materialize only to dissolve as another place came to mind. My stomach lurched as each place came in and out of focus. I was going to need some Dramamine if I didn't settle on one destination soon. I closed my eyes and focused on just my sister. I pictured her exactly as she was when I left her at the luncheon yesterday, laughing and smiling with her friends. I concentrated on nothing but Frankie until I could practically feel that gravitational pull she had. I didn't try to figure out where she was, deciding instead to let the between lead me to her. I followed the pulling sensation until I felt cold, hard concrete beneath me. I sat there for a second, letting my stomach settle.

I opened my eyes and cursed my sister.

Chapter Five

"Of all the places, damn it Frankie." I grumbled. It was bad enough that I had to bring her back to Beacon Hill and the dragon lady. "Make yourself scarce Conry. You aren't allowed in."

I crossed the street still baffled at how my sister ended up here. I took a deep breath and opened the door to The Daily Grind. I was about to go in when I realized Conry was still stuck to my side. I told him to stay, sit and lie down but he ignored all of my commands. I gave up. What's the worst that could happen, they'd toss me out? I was pretty sure that would happen regardless.

Conry evaporated as soon as I walked through the door. Cool! I knew he was there, I could still feel his breath on my hand. If we could manage to avoid bumping into anyone they'd never know my mystical dog was there.

Frankie looked up as soon as the little chime above the door rang out. "Maurin!" She exclaimed. "It took you long enough. I've had enough espresso to keep me awake for a week waiting for you."

I grimaced as she practically shouted my name. Every eye in the room was focused on me. I tried not to squirm under the scrutiny of so many unfriendly faces. "Frankie we need to go."

"You said you came here all the time. I thought you liked this place?" She whined. "I've been sitting here alone like a total loser hoping you'd show up."

"I'm giving up coffee." She raised a skeptical brow. "Fine, I haven't given up anything. I'm kind of banned from the Grind." I cut her off before she could ask me why. "Firstly, I used to come here alone all the time and I am not a loser. Secondly, we're not here to talk about me. I'm taking you home, let's go Frankie."

"Sit down Maurin. I'm not going home." She informed me.

"Fine, we can go somewhere else." She just crossed her arms and sat back in my favorite chair like an insolent child. I fought the urge to tip her out of the chair and plop down on the warn leathery cushions. Man I missed this place. "Did you hear what I said? We're leaving. My money's no good here."

"Well mine is. I gave that girl a fifty dollar tip. So sit down and order something so we can talk. I really need some sisterly advice." She was glaring at me, daring me with her eyes to argue. I remembered the skill with which she would throw a tantrum as a child and sensed we weren't far from a repeat performance.

I hesitantly sat down on the edge of the chair next to my sister, unwilling to get comfortable for fear of getting tossed out on my ass at any second. Before I could object Frankie was waving Amalie over to take my order. I didn't even bother looking over my shoulder to see if she was coming. I could hear hushed arguing from behind the counter.

"I saw Michael." I told her, in an effort to get the conversation moving so we could get the hell out of here before someone hexed me.

"You went to my apartment?" She seemed surprised to hear I made a point of seeing her fiancé or ex-fiancé as the case maybe. "He told you what happened?"

"I didn't really give him much choice." I laughed. "Look I'm the last person who should be giving advice, my life is far from normal. But people are going to start showing up at a wedding with no bride or groom in a couple hours. So if you really don't plan on being there you might want to give the priest a heads up."

I was about to lay on the guilt trip about how worried everyone was when Amalie came over with a cup of coffee and a croissant. I gave her a weak smile as she set them down on the little table in front of us. She didn't say anything, just smiled back and walked away. Peace offering or poison? She gave some guy who said something about Council whores not being welcome here the finger on her way back to the counter. Maybe it was safe to eat. I picked a corner of the croissant and popped it into my mouth. It turned to ash on my tongue. I passed on the coffee.

"I don't even care about the thing with Ashley. I mean I do but I wasn't entirely faithful either." Frankie blurted out as I debated wiping my tongue with a napkin.

Not wanting to give the asshole who hexed my food the satisfaction I ignored the foul taste in my mouth. "What?" I couldn't take it, I grabbed Frankie's coffee and swished it around in my mouth. "Does Michael know?"

"Yes." She frowned and reached for my cup. I handed hers over before the loser two tables down had a chance to hex it and waited for her to continue. "I told him after he told me about Ashley. She's been trying to break us up since they started that stupid study group. He told me he couldn't marry me with a lie like that between us. He's a better person than me because I had no intention of telling him what happened with his old roommate."

"His roommate? Who are you and what have you done with my sister? I mean honestly Frankie!" If she wasn't telling me I wouldn't have believed it.

"Don't judge me Maurin. You're not perfect. Care to tell me why you're getting banned from coffee houses now?" When I didn't elaborate she went on, "It was rush week, I had way too much to drink. It was just the one time and we both regretted it. He moved out at the end of the semester. Anyway none of that matters. I know Michael loves me."

"And you love him?" I asked, thoroughly confused and in need of confirmation.

"Of course I do. Don't be thick Maurin." She so reminded me of her mother when she said that.

"Help me out here Frankie, if you're both willing to over look your infidelities why did you take off?" Why couldn't we be having this conversation at Toil and Trouble? Why couldn't I be fighting a demon instead of having this conversation? I was so much better at that. At least that made sense. Bad guy hurts good guy, eliminate the bad guy. This on the other hand? I couldn't get a handle on why any of this was so Earth shattering or how they managed to stay together this long.

"He wants to move to Washington. He accepted the offer at some big firm without even talking to me about it. I had a flash of my life as the wife of a junior partner. I was already freaking out before he even mentioned Ashley. I don't care that he made a mistake. So did I. Our relationship is probably better for it. But I don't want to turn into mom. I can't." She looked like she was about to hyperventilate.

I obviously hadn't been spending enough time around norms because I was ready to get up and walk out. This whole conversation seemed ridiculous. I was really trying to see the severity of the situation but couldn't. "I think the odds of you turning into mom are far greater if you stay here. Do you want to marry Michael? Be honest."

She didn't hesitate. "Yes, more than anything just on my terms."

I sighed. We weren't getting anywhere. "I think the terms are covered under the vows."

"It's supposed to be a partnership. He didn't even ask me what I wanted." She said.

"And what would you have said if he asked?" I already knew the answer. She graduated in May and wanted to be an artist full time.

"Of course I would have said yes. I can paint anywhere. He took it for granted." She huffed.

"Did you try telling him that or did you assume he was going to turn you into the Stepford Wife mom dressed you up like yesterday?" I was getting irritated that all my answers seemed to be defending Michael when all I wanted to do was punch him in the face for cheating on my sister. It didn't matter that she cheated on him first. Not very rational, I know.

"So you think I should go through with it, the wedding, moving to DC?" She asked.

"I am not going to tell you what to do Frankie. You've got to make that decision for yourself but you already knew that." See I totally sucked at giving advice.

"I've got to go!" She jumped up and bolted for the door. "You better be at the church!"

"I think that was supposed to be my line." I called out.

I grabbed Frankie's cup of coffee as I got up, raising it to the jerkwad who referred to me as a Council whore. I could feel Conry beside me as I walked out. I took a swig of the now ice cold coffee as my dog materialized next to me. My taste buds were once again assaulted with bitter ash. Son of a bitch. I tossed the coffee in the trash can on the corner. With that "crisis" averted I could finally report back to the Council. I decided to go home and change first. Knowing Agrona she would keep me at the Council meeting well into the reception.

I was so glad Frankie didn't ask me to be a bridesmaid. I had no desire to spend the evening in the ankle length, pin straight and super tight pewter dresses she picked out. A dress like that was not designed for someone who was barely five foot two. The women's tux inspired suit I bought from Black Market fit perfectly. Just the right amount of cleavage was visible with the black strapless top, highlighted by the black crystal beadwork along the edge. I was a little concerned about the top but the woman at the store assured me the boning would help keep it in place. It would be just my luck to have a wardrobe malfunction. There was no way to hide my sword in this outfit but I managed to strap a dagger to each calf. Another reason I was grateful for pants. My hair was pulled up in a chignon and I finished off the look with a smoky eye and nude glossy lip. Three inch heels completed the outfit. Seeing it all together for the first time, I had to agree with the sales associate. I didn't need a fancy designer dress that I couldn't afford. Sometimes less is definitely more. I slipped on the jacket and took one last look at myself in the mirror before heading out to meet the Council with Conry in tow.

Chapter Six

The Council had recently taken ownership of a local burlesque club. Apparently, there was more than a little private dancing going on in the back rooms. Rule number one when running a club for norms and others in Salem, don't let the vampires drink the norms. Especially not for money. Seems the prior owner found out selling vampire bites for the sexual euphoria that follows was pretty lucrative. The Council didn't approve of that particular business venture so they were the proud new owners of Risqué. They went in fully intent on shutting the place down but after closer inspection they all agreed to keep it open. It wasn't the club that really interested the Council, it was the space below it. Once a speak easy during prohibition, the club beneath the club offered a neutral meeting ground for all factions of the Council and their constituents.

I knocked on the back door. A woman wearing a black tee shirt with the word security in bold white letters stretched across her chest opened the door. She gave me a hard once over before stepping aside. Some patrons might make the mistake of thinking they could take her on but I knew without even a hint of fang that she was a vampire. After giving me a quick pat down she was ready to take me downstairs.

"You come with me. The dog stays here." She motioned to someone I couldn't see, presumably to watch Conry.

"The *dog* is coming with me." I was trying to play nice. This was my first time at Risqué - most of the staff didn't know me. I let her frisk me but I was not going downstairs without Conry. If I had known this would be an issue, I would have told Conry to go stealth mode. They had already seen him so it was too late for that.

She was fast but not fast enough. She came at me, arm extended to grab me by my neck and shove me against the wall. With my left arm I struck out at the inside of her elbow, bending her arm. I threw my right shoulder into her chest using her momentum to flip her around and force her back against the bricks. If she was even half a century older that move wouldn't have worked but I've gone up against the equivalent of her great-great-great-well a lot of greats- grandmother and lived to talk about it. I could certainly handle this toddler.

"Must you always resort to violence Maurin?"

I didn't recognize the voice. Conry instinctively moved in front of me. I eased my weight off the bouncer and slowly turned around. My heart stopped. The bouncer's bright red lips curved up into a wicked grin. She caught the hiccup in my heartbeat and knew this particular fae scared the shit out of me. Aidan warned me about Kellen the first time I saw him at Mahalia's trial. I had seen him only twice since then but my skin crawled every time he looked at me. His power felt both familiar and foreign.

"You were instructed to bring her down immediately upon her arrival." His voice was calm but I could tell he was fuming inside. He gave the bouncer a look that practically had me quaking in my three-inch heels.

"She brought her dog. I told her he couldn't go down. She wouldn't cooperate." The bouncer explained in a rush.

"Is that how it happened Maurin? You refused to leave your guardian behind after being instructed to do so by our security?" It felt like a trick question - like no matter what I said the vampire would be punished. Something I was certain he would enjoy.

I glanced at the vampire who was daring me with her eyes to say otherwise. "I don't answer to security and Conry stays with me."

I could see the tension leave the vampire's body when I corroborated her story. She was safe from his wrath for now.

"Follow me. Everyone is waiting for you." Kellen extended a hand to Conry whose lips curled back in a snarl in response. He laughed and I broke out into a cold sweat. This fae's power was dangerously close to dark magic.

Conry fell in step beside me as we followed him down the stairway into the old speak easy part of the club. The room, once damp and dimly lit for drinking and gambling away from the watchful eyes of Johnny Law, was now a fully renovated bar decorated in full Gatsby grandeur. I took my place in front of Agrona who was sprawled glamorously across a chaise lounge. Kedehern sat on a stool with his back to the bar, elbows propped on the wooden top supporting him as he casually leaned back. My fae escort took his seat next to his brother on a velvet set tee. He didn't bother feigning interest.

"So tell me all the gory details. Did Roul make short work of Cash or did he toy with him for a while?" Agrona almost sounded excited.

It hadn't occurred to me that I would actually be breaking the news of Roul's death to the Council - report back on what I witnessed yes but I assumed they already knew about Roul. They always knew everything. Of course the two people who usually reported shifter activity to the Council were dead so....

"Actually," I cleared my throat when Agrona sat up. "Actually, he lost. The Salem pack belongs to Cash."

For the briefest moment I caught concern in Agrona's usually emotion less eyes. No remorse or sorrow, just concern. I knew it wasn't for the wolf pack. "Why didn't Olwyn inform us of Roul's death herself?"

"That would be hard to do since she's dead too." My throat was suddenly dry. I nodded toward Kedehern and the bar. She didn't object so I walked over to the bar as Kedehern poured me a drink.

"He killed the Omega?" Agrona was on the edge of her seat.

I slammed the, holy Hades, Wild Turkey and waited for the burn to pass before I spoke. "I killed her."

"You?" Agrona said surprised.

"You are a violent little creature, aren't you? Do tell Maurin, why did you slay the she-beast?" I had once again drawn the attention of the creepy, beautiful but creepy fae. He was suddenly very interested in the conversation. A chill ran down my spine and I fought not to shake it off.

I avoided looking at the fae, choosing instead to direct my response at Agrona. "She went insane the moment Cash killed Roul. She shifted. There was nothing left of Olwyn, her wolf had completely taken over. She attacked me. I had no choice."

"That isn't uncommon among the shifters. When one's mate dies they follow soon after. Most are put down. It takes a remarkably strong will to survive severing the mating bond." Kedehern explained as if he were giving a lecture on shifters and not discussing his former Councilman.

"It would seem there is yet another vacancy on the Council." Kellen looked to his brother. Neither spoke a word to the other but something had definitely passed between them.

"There are already two courts by my count among the fae. We are not creating a third here in Salem. The Wolves will keep their seat for now." Agrona snapped.

And there was the reason for the concern. Something was happening in faery and these two fae were looking to make a power play here in the Council.

"So, you vouch for the wolf then?" Kellen asked.

"I do not need to *vouch* for anyone. The last time I checked I was still head of this Council. You would be wise to remember that." Anger flushed Agrona's face with the blood of her last meal.

"The last time I checked this wasn't a dictatorship. You would be wise to remember that Carnage." There was a history between them - and certainly no love loss - if he was referring to her by her nickname. Maybe she fed on more than humans back in England. Kellen's ice blue eyes lasered in on me. "Be a good little girl and fetch the wolf."

I flicked my gaze to Agrona. I didn't know what Kellen was up to but something told me it wasn't good.

"You don't need to look to her for approval. As a councilman you answer to me as well." Muscles twitched in his jaw as he fought to control his temper. He ran his hands through his long pale blonde hair when he realized I saw it. When I made no move to get Cash his fair skin darkened to an almost sickly gray. "You seem reluctant. Perhaps I can persuade you."

Conry whimpered as he was painfully forced to heel at Kellen's feet. Shit. I tried not to flinch. If I wasn't careful I could find myself in faery with Mahalia and I had no desire to be stuck there with her as a cell mate and him as my jailer. Before I could tell him that I would find Cash I was hit with the weight of his magic. He was pulling from the between and force feeding it to me. The more I resisted the more he shoved into me. When my skin felt like it was about to split wide open, spilling the magic that made up the place between places all over their fancy carpet, I stopped fighting and let the between take me. I landed hard on my ass in the nothingness that was the between and focused on Cash just like I did when I was looking for my sister. I concentrated until I felt that familiar pull in my core and let it take me to Salem's new Alpha.

The pack was still on Winter Island. For the first time since learning how to move through realities I felt like I was going to throw up. I stopped a few feet away from the old hanger and tried to settle my stomach and my nerves. I hated leaving Conry behind.

"Who the fuck are you and how the fuck did you get here?" Someone growled behind me.

"Who the fuck are you?" was my answer. I heard the distinct sound of someone cocking a gun.

"Nolak put the gun down. Damn girl, are you trying to get yourself killed?" Cash called out from the doorway into the hanger.

"If you're not going to use that gun could you maybe put it away?" Healing bullet wounds was a bitch.

"Maurin this is Nolak. He's running security. Nolak the woman whose head you're contemplating blowing off is Maurin Kincaide." Cash walked toward us as he made introductions.

"That's all she had to say." Nolak grumbled as he lowered his gun and marched off.

"Next time try letting me know you're coming. What are you doing back here anyway?"

"I didn't have time to call ahead. Who's the muscle?" I asked.

"He's a friend from Boston." That was all the explanation I was going to get.

"Is he staying? I have to report that to SPTF remember?" It dawned on me then that at some point I would have to pay a visit to Masarelli to tell him there's a new Alpha in town.

"He's not staying. So, are you going to tell me why you came back here tonight? I thought you had a wedding to go to."

"I have one last Council errand to do tonight." I said.

"I take it that has something to do with me." Cash crossed his arms over his chest.

"I need to take you to the Council."

"Yeah, sure. I'm not doing anything important like burying two bodies, exerting my dominance over my new pack. No big deal." He sounded pretty pissed that I even suggested he leave tonight.

"Wasn't it you who said something about not blowing off Council responsibilities?" I tried using his argument against him.

"Yeah well if I had any that might work but since I don't the Council can wait." He was already walking away.

"As a councilman I'd say you have a serious obligation to them." I yelled at him.

"What?" He growled as he rounded on me. "I don't want a seat on the Council."

"Well too bad because Agrona is giving it to you and you're going to take it." I poked him in the chest, emphasizing each word.

"Like hell." He said.

"We don't have time for this crap. You're going to see the Council. The fae are looking to make a power play for the empty seat on the Council and Agrona's looking to use you to keep it from happening." I held out my hand hoping he would just come willingly. I'd drag him through the between if I had to.

"I don't want to get caught up in that political bullshit." Cash was looking at my hand like he would catch leprosy if he touched it.

"Well then you shouldn't have killed the last Alpha. We're leaving now so you might want to let someone know." I told him.

After stringing an impressive amount of curse words together he called for Tybalt and Nolak.

Cash filled his wolves in on where I was taking him and gave them instructions to finish the burial and to keep the pack on Winter Island until he got back. The ceremonial hunt could wait until then. I knew this was terrible timing. Cash needed to be here with the pack. Anytime a new Alpha comes to power by challenge he is vulnerable until the pack bond has taken hold - which is why most Alphas are challenged within days of taking over a pack. Unfortunately, we didn't have days. We needed to nip this Council shit in the bud.

I grabbed Cash's hand and started to pull us through the between. Nolak drew his gun and had it aimed center mass before Tybalt forced him to put it away. It wouldn't have mattered. There wasn't enough of my physical body left on Winter Island, by the time the first bullet shot from the barrel Cash and I would have been in the between. I didn't blame him for trying though. It's not every day some girl, far less physically intimidating than a werewolf, comes in and makes an Alpha disappear.

We were both breathing heavy when we got back to the Council. A wave of nausea threatened to empty the contents of my stomach for the second time. Which wasn't much so I would have just ended up dry heaving. I took another deep breath and tried to force the feeling away. I hadn't eaten anything since, well I couldn't remember. I was drained. Cash was obviously able to pull a little strength from the pack because he wasn't even close to shifting this time. He looked like he had a mild case of motion sickness but this was definitely his best reaction to the between so far. It was my worst. I needed to refuel; I was using too much energy.

"So, this is the new Alpha? A fine specimen wouldn't you agree brother?" Kellen asked the fae to his side.

"Much better than the beast at your feet." Ian said eyeing up the werewolf across from him.

I could tell that Conry was still being forced to stay there and fighting against Kellen was causing him a lot of pain.

"I don't know what's going on but I do know that if you don't get your fucking hands off my dog you and I are going to have a serious problem." I gave a whistle for Conry to come when I was sure Kellen had released him.

My guardian stood and slowly walked across the room. He barely made it to me before his massive body collapsed at my feet. I knelt down next to him and rubbed his side. It took all I had not to unsheath one of my daggers and fling it at Kellen's head. I needed to keep my cool and let this play out. I still didn't know what the hell was going on or why he could shove magic through me - not to mention control Conry.

Out of the corner of my eye I noticed Cash's hands shaking. Agrona and Kedehern saw it too because they were moving in on the fae. The air was suddenly thick with magic. I could feel my hair standing on end from the static charge.

A growl formed in the back of Cash's throat. "You aren't going to force me to shift." Cash was pulling hard on the pack to keep Kellen's magic at bay. It said a lot about him as an Alpha that he could do that so soon after the challenge.

My hand instinctively went for one of my daggers. I slid it from its sheath and let it fly. It buried itself to the handle in Kellen's shoulder. He staggered back as blood darkened the sleeve of his gray tunic. Cash rolled his shoulders and cracked his neck as he stalked toward the fae. Agrona and Kedehern moved in for the kill, each sliding behind one of the brothers. Held in the vampire version of a rear naked choke the fae were forced to concede defeat.

"So the fae think they can strong arm the Council into doing its bidding? Be sure to pass this along to your queen for me." Agrona sank her fangs into Kellen's neck. When she had her fill of faerie blood she released him. He crumpled at her feet. "Interesting. You don't speak for your queen." She nudged his limp body with the toe of her Jimmy Choo. "Perhaps I should have a talk with her myself. When she chose you to represent your people this side of faerie I don't think this is what she had in mind. It certainly won't gain you any allies in the fight against the darkness creeping through the faerie mound."

Kedehern let Ian go without spilling or drinking a drop of his blood. He scrambled to collect his brother and return to faerie. Feeling confident we had gained the upper hand we let them go.

"You knew they were going to do that if Cash won the challenge, didn't you?" I asked.

"Of course I did. It's my job to know." She went to the bar, took a cocktail napkin off the counter and dabbed her mouth. "I've never cared for the taste of faerie blood, gives me a terrible hangover."

"I recall a time when you thirsted for nothing else." Kedehern laughed.

"I didn't say I didn't enjoy the power boost." Agrona's eyes were brighter than I had ever seen them.

"Why didn't you just drain them when you found out what they were up to?" I was too exhausted to put it together on my own and still had a wedding reception to get to. I missed the ceremony as predicted.

"That wouldn't have been nearly as much fun or had the desired effect. Rook takes pawn." She replied.

"Kellen is a descendant of the animal clan. If he was successful in dominating our new Alpha he would have control over the Council by majority. I don't think Roul would have passed the test. It was an impressive display of power on your part." Kedehern nodded to Cash.

"You think he'll just stop?" Cash asked.

"Things work a little differently in faerie. Ruthless and often deadly politics rule the mound. This was mild compared to how things are usually done." Kedehern explained.

"But what was the point? And how does him being from the animal clan give him the ability to shove magic down my throat like that?" I really wanted an answer to the magic part.

"The Fae are in trouble. Their magic is failing. Most of their power comes from nature. The rate at which man reproduces, the growth of cities and harvesting of natural resources has been devastating to the fae. Some have turned to darker magic to survive and it is spreading through the mound, contaminating it and the creatures who inhabit it. Kellen hoped to overpower us tonight and force us to help them. As for you? I think he was borrowing power from the queen. Though it might be wise to follow up with your father on that front. The most important thing is tonight we showed the fae that while they are growing weaker we are growing stronger. Even you Maurin, were able to strike a blow against them." He said.

"You don't think this will be a problem going forward? How the hell are you supposed to get anything done with the fae trying to force you into submission every chance they get?" Cash barked.

"I believe the correct question is how are we going to get anything done. You are a councilman after all." Agrona laughed. "Tonight was a battle of wills, which we won. If the fae want our help cleaning up their mound they will have to ask for it. They won't cause any more trouble on the Council."

With that the meeting was concluded. Cash wasn't just the new alpha of the Salem pack but a councilman as well - reluctantly filling the vacancy he created. I offered to jump him back to his pack but he opted for use of the Council car service. Being a councilman did have its perks.

Chapter Seven

I made it to the reception before the dj announced Mr. and Mrs. Calhoun. After giving Conry explicit institutions to stay in the lobby doing his invisibility trick I grabbed my place card on the way into the elegant ballroom of the Liberty Hotel. I finally found my table and took my seat. It wasn't with the rest of the family but hey it wasn't the kids table either.

Frankie and Michael walked in to a thunderous applause, the entire room oblivious to the premarital drama that ensued earlier in the day. She looked happy as he spun her onto the dance floor for their first dance as husband and wife. Michael caught sight of me as he twirled my sister and I could practically see the sweat beading on his forehead. I didn't foresee a lot of holidays at the Calhoun's. Appetizers that I didn't have to serve this time came and went. Filet mignon was served followed by chocolate soufflé. Followed by several top shelf drinks from the open bar. Couples danced and moved about the room socializing. I was still sitting at my table polishing off yet another amaretto sour when a hand extended in front of me.

"Nobody puts baby in a corner."

"I'm not in a corner but I am a little concerned that you were able to pull that movie line." I let Cash take my hand and lead me out to the dance floor. "I should warn you I can't dance."

"Sure you can. It's like fighting, imagine you're in a ring moving around your opponent. And for the record it was my mother's favorite movie. It's iconic."

"Iconic is not the word I would use." I laughed. "So councilman what brings you to the social event of the season? Don't you have a ceremony of your own to attend?"

"Yeah, I do but..." He stopped leading me around the dance floor. I caught that same look I saw him give Tybalt when they applied the Wolfsbane.

"What? What is it?" Something told me I really didn't want to know the answer.

"I needed to be sure." He hesitated.

"This dance is about to be exactly like a fight because I am going to knock you on your ass if you don't spit it out." I wouldn't make good on the threat in the middle of my sister's wedding reception and Cash knew it but he had the good sense to pretend I would.

"I needed to make sure the Wolfsbane was working." He blurted out.

"What? Why the hell didn't you do that before? Like at Risqué? It would have been a hell of a lot easier to cover up me shifting and attacking a pole dancer than an entire wedding party!" I managed to yell in a whisper.

"It's not like I haven't had a lot going on. You haven't displayed any signs of shifting. I just needed to be sure." He said.

"If I haven't shown any signs then why are you here?" I asked.

"Because you're in a room full of Boston's elite and I'd rather you not try to eat the bridal party in front of them." He smirked.

"Nice. While most days I wouldn't mind feeding my mother to a pack of wolves, I actually like my sister." I teased.

"The full moon is at its peak. I think it's safe to say you're not going to go all big, bad wolf on the bride and groom." Cash started moving us around the dance floor again. "You just heal so fast and I was second guessing myself. I just wanted to be sure you were alright."

"And why wouldn't she be alright?"

"Aidan." His name escaped my lips in a breathy whisper. He looked amazing in Armani.

"Mind if I cut in?" Aidan held out his hand.

I took his hand and let him pull me out of Cash's arms and into his. I think Cash said something about calling him if I needed anything but I was too lost in Aidan's eyes to hear it.

"You're back early." I said as he led us in a waltz. The dance was a little slow for the music but I wasn't complaining as long as I was this close to him.

"I followed every possible lead in Iceland. Unfortunately, they all pointed in one direction. Salem." I thought he would elaborate but instead he abruptly changed the subject. "I went to your apartment and you weren't there. It occurred to me that you might actually attend your sister's wedding. I had hoped to be your plus one but I see I'm too late and you've already found an escort for the evening." Aidan actually looked worried.

"We already had this conversation." I cut off his response with a kiss. I didn't care if people were staring. His lips parted, opening his mouth enough for me to slip my tongue inside. I couldn't get enough of him. I ran my tongue along his teeth, intentionally pressing against a fang causing just the smallest drop of blood to well up. It was enough to get a small groan out of him. We kissed until I couldn't breathe any more. I nibbled his bottom lip as he pulled away for me to catch my breath.

"Mmm, I love the way you smell. Vanilla and cinnamon with just a hint of tangerine." He nuzzled into my neck. "And wolf. I'd rather you not have his scent on you." He dipped me causing my bodice to ride up and expose the claw marks on my stomach. He jerked me up and pressed me tight against his body. "I can't leave you alone can I?"

I didn't know what to say that wouldn't send him over the edge. Before I could tell him I was fine and it was no big deal - which would have been the understatement of the year since I was a hairs breath away from going fury every full moon - he left me alone on the dance floor. Only the couples closest to us saw him move. One woman let out a little gasp as her husband quickly fox trotted her away from me. I knew he went after Cash. I needed to find my sister and say good night. Which was code for goodbye. She would slip into her new life and I would forever slip out of this one.

I tapped Michael on the shoulder. He stopped dancing and for a second his heart stop beating. I raised my hands in mock surrender. "I just came to say goodnight."

Michael seemed to deflate as he let out a heavy sigh when he realized I wasn't going to choke him again. Frankie slipped out of his arms and gave me a tight hug. "I love you."

"I love you too." It was easier than saying goodbye even though we both knew it was. I squeezed her back and headed out after Aidan and Cash. Conry was on my heels as soon as I hit the lobby.

I found them in the hotel bar Clink, aptly named since it utilized the original jail cells in its decor. The bar was empty since my mother had basically reserved the entire hotel but if this conversation continued in here we were going to end up behind bars for real.

"I leave her side for two days, two dammed days and you let her get mauled by a bloody werewolf?" Aidan had Cash by the throat.

Cash was keeping remarkably cool despite Aidan's aggression. "If you're looking for someone to blame you can start with your boss. She's the one who sent Maurin to witness the challenge."

"It looks more like she refereed the fucking challenge. You damn near disemboweled her! Is she infected? Is she?" Aidan was angrier than I had ever seen him. His Irish accent was so thick I had a hard time understanding him. He slammed Cash against the wall.

"She's right here and she's fine." I said, apparently talking to myself.

"We gave her Wolfsbane. I just needed to be sure.." Cash was trying to explain but Aidan cut him off.

"Wolfsbane? You could have killed her. I should just break your neck and be done with you." Aidan squeezed his throat a little tighter.

"Killing an Alpha is tantamount to war fanger." Cash pulled a little more power from the pack and broke free of his grip. "As your councilman I would advise against laying your cold, dead hands on me again or I'll have you organizing blood drives for the rest of your miserable existence." He shoved Aidan back, knocking over two of the tables.

Aidan rocketed off the floor. I jumped in between them before he got his hands on Cash again. Standing in the middle of a pissed off vampire and werewolf probably wasn't the smartest idea I'd ever had. I'd have better luck trying to stop a head on collision with two eighteen wheelers. Conry tugged my pant leg in an attempt to pull me out from between them. I threw my arms out slamming a palm into each chest and prayed my wrists didn't snap.

"The bar is closed for a private party." A hotel employee came in expecting to chase out some of the local bar hoppers. He took one look at us and the upturned tables and started yelling. "Hey, what the hell's going on in here? Get the hell out of here before I call the cops!" Cash and Aidan were each waiting for the other to back down and I was too busy trying to keep them apart. The guy grabbed a cell phone out of his pocket. SPTF was going to come in like gang busters if I didn't get us out of here. Before the bellhop could dial nine I grabbed a hold of Aidan and Cash and jumped us back to my apartment.

We landed hard on my living room floor in a tangled heap. It was by far the sloppiest jump I'd made to date. They jumped up ready to go at each other for real. I should have picked Cash's apartment. They could break as much of his shit as they wanted. I swallowed back the five star meal that was working its way back up and pushed myself off the floor.

"Enough!" I gave Aidan a hard shove. "If it wasn't for Cash you'd be out shopping for chew toys right now! So knock it off!"

"Call off your dog Maurin." Conry had Cash backed up to the wall separating the living room from the kitchen.

"Not unless you two are going to play nice. It may not be much but I'd appreciate it if you didn't destroy everything I own trying to beat the shit out of each other."

Aidan eased back a little. "He could have killed you. He couldn't possibly know what effects Wolfsbane will have on you."

"It had exactly the effect I hoped. It stopped her from becoming infected." Cash had relaxed a little too since Conry backed off.

With each of them in their respective corners Conry and I had a better chance of keeping the situation under control.

"Yeah well that's not all it did. She stinks to high hell like dog and in case you didn't notice she's having some kind of reaction. She's sick, weak." At least Aidan wasn't yelling anymore.

"Are you sick? Why didn't you say anything?" Cash started to close the distance between us.

I shook my head, stopping him where he was. It was better if there was still a little space between them - and me. "I've practically thrown up every time I've moved through the between since you gave me the Wolfsbane. Maybe that's why Kellen was able to shove that much power into me?" I didn't expect anyone to know the answer to that.

"Kellen? What the fuck does he have to do with this?" Aidan had a hold of my forearms and gave them a little squeeze. "I told you to steer clear of him."

"She can't steer clear of a council member anymore than you can." Cash leaned arrogantly against my wall as he reminded Aidan of his new position.

I shot him a nasty look over my shoulder. "Not helping. You need to get back to your pack and I need to talk to Aidan."

"In other words get the fuck out." Aidan definitely wasn't thrilled with Cash's sudden rise to power in the super natural community.

"Any side effects from the Wolfsbane should be gone by tomorrow. If you're still having problems let me know. You've got my number. See you at the next council meeting fanger." Cash let himself out.

Aidan dropped to his knees, his face pressed against my midsection, as soon as the door clicked shut. "You're going to be the death of me Maurin."

I ran my fingers through his hair. I was in so deep where Aidan was concerned. He looked up at me with eyes filled with concern. He unbuttoned my jacket and slid it off my shoulders. His fingers grazed the edge of the scars that weren't covered by my top. I unzipped the side zipper and pulled the bodice over my head. With just a strapless bra covering my upper body Aidan had a full view of exactly how much damage had been done to my stomach.

"If you had…. If they couldn't…" He couldn't seem to find the words.

"I'm fine." At least I thought I was.

"One of these days you might not be able to say that." He sighed, giving me goose bumps as his breath danced across my stomach. "I need to know exactly what happened with the Council, with Kellen."

"Right now?" I asked seductively as I slid down into his lap.

His mouth crushed mine, devouring me like a man on the brink of starvation. "I suppose it can wait."